For Alex

Copyright © 1997 by Sandy Nightingale

The rights of Sandy Nightingale to be identified as the author and illustrator of this work
have been asserted by her in accordance with the Copyright, Designs and Patents Act, 1988.
First published in Great Britain in 1997 by Andersen Press Ltd., 20 Vauxhall Bridge Road, London SW1V 2SA.
Published in Australia by Random House Australia Pty., 20 Alfred Street, Milsons Point, Sydney, NSW 2061.
All rights reserved. Colour separated in Italy by Fotoriproduzioni Grafiche, Verona.
Printed and bound in Italy by Grafiche AZ, Verona.

10   9   8   7   6   5   4   3   2   1

British Library Cataloguing in Publication Data available.
ISBN 0 86264 739 8

This book has been printed on acid-free paper

THE WITCH'S SPELL

Written and illustrated by
Sandy Nightingale

A

Andersen Press • London

One afternoon,
Witch Widdershins and
her gang were flying
very low in the sky. They
were looking for a new place
to live.

"That looks promising!" screamed
the witch, pointing to a tumbledown cottage,
and down she zoomed to land in the garden.
"Lumpet, Sniggle, get to work!"

They rushed inside the cottage and
chased out all the little creatures who were
living there.

They felt very tough and scary and were horribly pleased with themselves.

"I like it here," Widdershins decided, looking round. "Lumpet, Sniggle, unpack everything and get me my tea. This is just the place to work on my greatest spell."

And she sat down, with Grimstone as a footstool, to think about it.

Early next morning, Widdershins wrapped herself in her magic shawl and got to work.

"This spell," she announced, "will destroy all the pretty, soppy things in the garden. I'm going to make everything horrible, dark and grotty which is just how we like it!"

Unfortunately, spells can be rather surprising.

Widdershins kept them hard
at work for days and days. Then she threw
open the front door to see if the spell was
working.

They all blinked in the bright sunlight.

"Look, Leader," croaked Lumpet excitedly,
"all the leaves have gone brown and
crunchy."

"And these silly flowers are fading," cried
Sniggle.

"Ah ha!" cackled the Witch. "It's a good
start, but back to work! I need a stronger
spell!"

All sorts of peculiar things
went into the bubbling cauldron —
spiders, beetles, and the blackest ink,
which Widdershins thought would make
the sky darker.

"I hate that stupid sun," she whinged.
"It makes my head ache."

Several weeks later, the spell was ready
to be tested again.

This time Widdershins flung open the shutters.

When the smoke had cleared, they peered hopefully around the garden.

"Hmm," pondered the witch, "not bad, but there's still too much colour."

Then she had a brilliant idea.

"Bring me bleach, bring me washing powder! And don't forget the stain remover," she demanded. "That'll do it! Back to work! I need a stronger spell."

The next time Widdershins opened the door, the whole garden was white and it was freezing cold.

"Look, Leader," yowled Grimstone, "you can make funny shapes with this white stuff."

"I must have overdone the bleach," screamed Widdershins. "This is no good, this is *pretty!* Fetch soot, fetch boot polish! Bring crows' feathers and squashed flies! Back to work! I need a stronger spell!"

At long last the spell was ready.

Widdershins flung open the door. The sight that met her eyes made her gasp in delight. The sky was dark and angry, lightning flashed, thunder rolled, and the wind howled.

She grabbed her cloak and danced out into the pouring rain.

"Success at last!" she screamed triumphantly. "My greatest work is complete!"

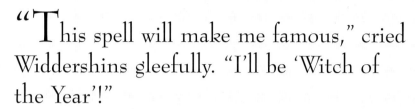

"This spell will make me famous," cried Widdershins gleefully. "I'll be 'Witch of the Year'!"

All the excitement made them very tired.

"We need a good long sleep," yawned the Witch, "and then I'll write my spell out neatly." So she set the alarm clock for half past April and they all went to bed.

"I won't thank anyone, because I did it all myself," muttered Widdershins as she fell asleep.

WITCH of the YEAR

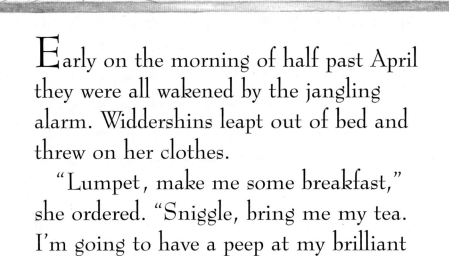

Early on the morning of half past April they were all wakened by the jangling alarm. Widdershins leapt out of bed and threw on her clothes.

"Lumpet, make me some breakfast," she ordered. "Sniggle, bring me my tea. I'm going to have a peep at my brilliant spell."

She strode across the dark room and flung open the shutters.

Instantly Spring sunshine flooded into the dusty cottage. Outside, butterflies fluttered and bees buzzed amongst the beautiful flowers.

Widdershins gasped, she gawped, she jumped through the window and stamped on the daisies in a fearful temper.

"What's this?" she shrieked in disbelief. "What has happened to my wonderful spell?"

W iddershins was so mad she nearly exploded.

Wailing like a banshee, she plunged back into the cottage and snatched up her broomstick. Then she shot up the chimney in a cloud of black soot. The gang just had to cling on as best they could.

They were never heard of again, and everyone else lived very happily ever after.